World of Reading

P9-DDC-557

THIS IS HULK

Adapted by Chris "Doc" Wyatt

Illustrated by Ron Lim and Rachelle Rosenberg

Based on the Marvel comic book series The Avengers

MARVEL

Los Angeles
New York

marvelkids.com

© 2015 MARVEL

Printed in the United States of America
First Edition, February 2015
1 3 5 7 9 10 8 6 4 2
G658-7729-4-14360
ISBN 978-1-4847-1658-8

SUSTAINABLE
FORESTRY
INITIATIVE

Certified Chain of Custody
Promoting Sustainable Forestry

www.sfiprogram.org
SFI-01415

The SFI label applies to the text stock

This is Hulk.

The Hulk is the strongest!
The Hulk is the biggest!

Hulk gets mad when bad guys try
to hurt good people.
He protects good people.

The madder the Hulk gets,
the stronger he gets.

The Hulk likes to say
"HULK SMASH"!
He is very good
at smashing things.

Hulk looks different
from other heroes.
Some people think
he is a monster.

The Hulk is sad when people treat him like a monster.

Yet the Hulk still protects people.

He even helps the ones
who are mean to him.

The Hulk is not always strong.

Sometimes he is Bruce Banner.
Bruce Banner is a scientist.

One day, before he was the Hulk, Bruce was testing a bomb.

Oh, no!
Someone walked into the test!

Bruce had to help.

He jumped in.
He saved the boy.
But he got blasted!

The blast turned Bruce
into the Hulk!

At first Bruce was scared.
He looked like a monster.

He found out the Hulk
can be good, too.
The Hulk can be a hero!

Whenever Bruce gets very mad,
he grows big and strong.

He turns into the Hulk!

Evildoers should fear the Hulk.

Good people do not have to worry.

An army general
wants to stop the Hulk.

But he will not.

Now the Hulk helps the Avengers.

The Hulk lives in Avengers Tower.

The Hulk and Thor
are best friends.

With the Avengers or alone,
the Hulk is always a Super Hero!